EUGENE WILLIAMS

Easter Island Sorta is a hilarious story about an average joe to say the least, that what's to know everything about the Island he has dreamed of visiting all his life without leaving Cleveland. Also you read a hilarious stories about a crazy cowboy and a golfing tell to end all golfing stories and on you go to meet the big red hat society like you never seen before.

Dedication:

Elizabeth Ann & Emily Grace

And everyone that's been to Easter Island if only through a television program, or magazine article this story for you, and of course the people of Cleveland Ohio.

EUGENE WILLIAMS

Ever since I was knee high to grasshopper, I wanted to pack my bags and dash off to Easter Island. Well maybe not dash off. At forty-nine and sixty pounds' overweight, I don't dash off anywhere except maybe to the john. However, you get my meaning. As I was saying there is something magical about a place in the middle of nowhere where for some unknown reason, someone has decided to erect giant stone figures all wearing stone hats perched on their heads while staring out across the sea. Gives me goose bumps every time I think about it.

You see some people dream about following in the footsteps of Bob Newhart, moving to Vermont opening a country Inn, and writing how-to-fix it books. Some people want to be astronauts, fly off to Mars and discover something no one has discovered before, and possibly live there as opposed to Cleveland. Actually, most of us just want to be left alone.

I fall in the all three categories, but for some weird reason I want to go and check out Easter Island if only for no other reason than just to satisfy my own curiosity that there really is such a place. I suppose I could just take the word of those more inclined to know these things.

Being that I was born a curious nature, I like to ask around, kind of get the feel-if you know what I mean-before I swallow the whole hook, line and sinker. Now I have read two maybe three articles about the place. Watched a television show, a documentary made in 1964, and have asked my neighbor his opinion. He is one of those people who just wants to be left alone.

So I decided rather than talk to someone half asleep all the time, I would seek out an expert on the matter-rather than swallow the whole hook, line and sinker.

EUGENE WILLIAMS

I began my first real expose' into the mystery of Easter Island by combing through the yellow pages, the only book I had close by my Lazy Boy, that and the T.V guide, which I had already given a careful examination.

I figured since my wife was visiting her mother for the weekend, I would take this time to research Easter Island; maybe with some newfound insight on the place she would take me more serious on the subject. Up till now whenever I bring it up, she takes off to her mother's house. I bring it up a lot.

My wife is also one of those people that just wants to be left alone. Moreover, her mother can't leave anyone alone. I figured somewhere between the Doctor and Lawyer ads, I could find an expert on Easter Island. This approach pretty much got me nowhere at first.

I realized I was going about it all wrong. They would only be of help if one of the stone figures fell on me. I needed to check out one of those New Age weirdo book places that specialize in stone faces and people with stone hats on. I found what I was looking for, an ad that read.

*Books and Stone Statues of Unsolved Mysteries. Visit our in house expert on Solving the Unsolvable.*

Thought the ad was a bit much, with all the little statues and weird symbol things, Nevertheless, like a mouse to cheese, I was caught in the trap of salesmanship.

After about an hour of procrastination, and judge Judy, I retrieved a Diet Coke from the refrig and poured it into my Big Gulp cup, jumped into the old Rambler Ambassador, turned the key five or six times until the starter finely caught the flywheel, peeling off a couple more teeth in the process. A puff of oily exhaust coughed out the back and I was almost ready to go, but first I popped in a David Allen Coe 8- track and wondered when was the last time my wife called me by my name.

My neighbor looked up as I was out the driveway, pulling his Dundee hat over his eyes, long enough to see it was only me. Satisfied my Rambler wasn't being stolen, he briefly gave me a wave of sorts and fell back too asleep in his lawn chair, leaning against an old water heater.

Amazing how he does that, more amazing is that the city lets him? Keep the water heater that is, Can't do much about him sleeping in the front yard. I waved back and slowly back out my driveway, with my yellow page phone book on my lap. That proved quite annoying very quickly, kind of like your dog sitting on your lap. You put up with the little fella, knowing full well the minute you have to slam on the brake pedal, you're going to go searching around the floor broad for the little fella, who's usually stuck under the gas pedal whimpering looking at you. Like what did you do that for?

Naturally you've cause a mile and a half traffic jam behind you, all on account of doing something just for the sake of doing it. Everyone honks their horns at the same time, and to make matter worst, some nearsighted little old man in a Continental with a twisted toupee, gives you the bird for good measure.

Therefore, I decided to forgo a headache from searching for the phone book in the middle of traffic, by laying it across the passenger's seat.

I made sure the New Age bookstore ad was angled just right, so I could glance down at it every minute or two-just to make sure I had the correct address.

Satisfied that I what I was reading was really what I was reading. I thought about closing the book before I drove into the path of a semi-truck or train.

Nevertheless, I knew I would need to reference the ad at least ten more times, before I got to where I was going. So I tried to ignore it. Amazing how you can't do that. After about twenty minutes of side street navigation, I finally ended up on highway 6. Hugging Lake Erie as I drove on, without much thought to the rocky shoreline, I did however scan the area for anglers, never knowing when someone might pull a big one upon to the rocks. I gave the area the once over again couldn't afford to miss the exit sign for East 55th street. According to my ad this New Age place was located near the Cleveland State University, which figured about right.

So I thought for a minute; maybe I should look for the Cleveland State University exit instead. While I thought about that, a sunbather distracted me momentarily and I noticed the Cleveland State University exit sign go right by me. I was back to looking for the exit sign for East 55th street.

I drove on without a care in the world. Satisfied no one was going to catch any fish today: too hot and too many snags along this section. I should know I spent many days on those rocks thanks to my wife and her mother.

Out of the clear blue a massive plane coming in for a landing at Burke Lakefront Airport nearly tossed old faithful my vehicle into oncoming traffic, which, of course, would have ruined my day and perhaps a few sunbathers as well.

You've never quite prepared for a jetliner two hundred feet from your window with a group of Japanese tourist waving at you as the fly by at a hundred miles per hour. No matter how many times you experience it, it scares the living crapola out of you every time.

I held on to Old faithful and rode the storm out; she fared better than I or the phone book. The shock waves from the plane were more than the phone book could handle. Leaning over my Big Gulp on the transmission hump caddie was no easy chore in the middle of traffic, but I had to retrieve the phone book from the floor broad. Man's gotta be able to keep one eye on the road and the other on his Big Gulp. Amazing the book was still on the ad page and not a drop spilled.

   I finally reached my exit a little shaken, but I had been through too much to turn around now. I drove on down East 55th street until I saw an old castle like brick building with a flashing red sign that said *We Read Palms* overhanging the road. Another smaller sign, made up to look like the one in the phone book, that said *"Books and stone Statues of Unsolved Mysteries."*

   Neither me nor Old faithful wanted to pull into driveway, but both of us had been through too much to turn around now.

   I gave a little extra gas, jumped over a speed bump, and settled into a vacant spot as far away from the entrance as I could find. Pushed my hair up under my baseball cap, what little I had on the side, that is. A quick look in the rearview mirror and I was ready.

   Now when you go into someplace for the first time-business or job interview doesn't matter much-you feel a little unsettled. Being I was about to go in search of unsolved mysteries in a business that also read palms didn't help matters. Now I seen Miss Clowee and Dione Warwick on television. Not that I believe in all that, but the phone company did tell me, I couldn't use my sister as an excuse any more to get out of paying the psychic hot line bill. Therefore, I had an idea of what I was getting myself into. A vague idea but an idea all the same. Moreover, it really was my sister sort of.

   Like a magnet, I had to find Easter Island and this was just as good a place as any. I figured if these New Age weirdos didn't know then nobody did; after all, what did the ad say In-house expert or something or other. I took a long pull on my Big Gulp, set it back in its caddie, then looked about to make sure there wasn't anybody around that might know me. Didn't need to explain what I was doing here to anybody, not that it was anyone's business.

I made sure my blue red checkered flannel shirt was tucked into my Dickies. Brushed off the left toe of my imitation calf skin work boots on my right calve, gave a tug on my belt just enough to hold my gut back a bit, and headed into the place like I owned it.

They say first impressions tell the story. Indeed, they were right. I never, ever, saw anything quite like this place. Beads and feathers and mirrors and spinning globes and lights everywhere, it was amazing.

After my eyes adjusted to the dimmer light, and I was sure I wasn't going to get a migraine, I stood there in the middle of the room trying to figure out which way to go.

Left were book-and records and magazines and posters. Giant statues of Demons and Angels and monkeys and bats were in the middle of the room. Next to those was a huge silver bowl with some blue haired middle age weirdo lady in a white toga spinning a glass ball in it. The faster she spun it, the more noise it made and the more she seemed to enjoy it.

I paused for a second to admire a half lion and half goat statue; it appeared as if the creature was holding a book to a kneeling mother and her child was playing with pieces of rocks or something.

Looking to my right was a wall containing perhaps as many as a hundred African masks, one that said *authentic Zulu warrior headdress.*

I tried to take in the whole picture but it was becoming too much too fast. There were perhaps a thousand mask everywhere. Moreover, the handful of people in the place, with exception of the spinning ball lady, were looking directly at me.

One young woman in a particular had purple hair, rings coming out of her nose and her bottom lip of all places. She started doing stretching exercises right next to the lion-goat statue. It was all too much too soon.

   This was nothing like standing in line at the unemployment office, I tell you nothing at all. I felt like I was going to fall over right there, you know kina weak in the stomach.

   The same feeling you get when you leave the horse track broke and you can't think of a good excuse to tell your wife what happened to your unemployment check. Not that that's happened to me, mind you.

   Nevertheless, I tugged on my belt, brushed by a skinny young man, I think, and headed for what looked like the main counter. I nearly made it to the counter when a voice seemed to appear from nowhere and said, "May I help yoooyou." The voice just echoed off the walls.

   I looked around at everyone looking at me, and then I heard it again. 'May I help yoooyou?" That's when I noticed a skinny tall fella with horn rim glasses holding a silver mike in his hands staring at me.

   I was transfixed by the strange looking fella in his white doctor's coat with a peacock feather cap on, repeating, "can I help yoooyou" repeatedly.

   Then I got irritated when I thought about how silly this whole mike and peacock feather thing was. I tugged on my belt and headed straight for him and his annoying hat as if I owned the place.

   "Stop that," I said looking him straight in the peacock feather.

   "Good day, sir, we are glad to see you have selected our store to do your shopping, anything in particular I may help you with?"

Amazing he didn't even stop to breathe all the way through that. Then he held his mike up and said. "can I help yoooyou."

I wanted to turn around and leave right then, but I had come too far now and Easter Island was on my mind. So I just smiled and came right out with it.

"I would like to know about Easter Island," I said

He sat his mike down, took off his cap, and eyed me for a minute, sizing me up I think. On the other hand, perhaps no one had ever asked him this question before, I wasn't sure. The skinny doctor just looked at me didn't blink, just looked at me.

"Absolutely fascinating," he said

I held my ground, not sure how to respond to this, so I just came right out with it. "What?"

"Your shirt," he said then continued grinning at me. "Absolutely fascinating, but to answer your question: first you must tell me what is it you would like to know about Easter Island."

I could tell we were on the right track now. I could talk to this fella. So I tugged on my belt again and tried to formulate something in my mind to say. He waited, playing with his peacock feather as he eyed me. I took a deep breath and came right out with it. "As long as I can remember I have always wanted to go to that Island and check out the statues. I can't put my finger on it, I just think they're interesting."

"No you don't," he said staring at the spinning ball lady. That wasn't the answer I was looking for, but at least we were talking.

"No I don't what." I said.

"No you don't think there're interesting. They are calling out to you, they want you to understand them." It was my turn. "No they don't".

"Yes they do," He said back, look at the spinning ball lady.

I didn't like this fella anymore, but I had come too far now to turn around and leave. Figuring that nothing from nothing leaves nothing, I said "okay have it your way, so what can you tell me about them?"

"About what?"

Somewhere between "yes they do" and "no they don't." this fella forgot what we were talking about. I figured I would try a different approach." Can I talk to your-in-house-expert?" I was starting to lose my patients with doc Peacock.

"I am him." he said.

Just as I about to turn and leave, he picked up his mike and starting telling everyone to gather round, he was about to answer a question. To my amazement even the spinning ball lady stopped doing what she was doing and walked over, leaning against me. I moved away just enough hoping she would my meaning, but she didn't. she moved with me.

"People, I will be speaking about Easter Island today. Let me introduce you, your name please."

"I'd rather not say." I said. The last thing in the world I wanted was these people to know who I was.

In the meantime, I was trying to keep Miss spinning ball from falling over.

I realized my not telling them my name made me appear pretty rude, but everyone thought I'd given the right answer, imagine that.

They all started clapping lightly, smiling at me. I felt honored in a silly kind of way. Nevertheless, I held my ground and the spinning ball lady up, and waited like everyone else for what doctor peacock feather hat was going to say. It didn't take long.

"Absolutely fascinating," he said eyeing me with a huge grin on his face.

"Now that everyone is totally unaware of who you are, let me begin."

I wasn't sure what he was going to say, but whatever it was, the rest of these people seemed quite happy about the whole affair. Everyone crowded in just a little too close for comfort as far as I was concerned. Nothing like the unemployment line. I tell you that much. He began by folding his well-manicured hands in front of him sissy like, eyeing me and began with:

"Easter Island, as most of you are aware, is nothing more than a volcanic outcropping 14 miles long by 7 miles wide. It is located some 2000 miles off the coast of South America and about 1100 miles from the nearest Polynesian Island, that being Pitcairn, which was made famous by those cut-throat mutineers on the HMS Bounty in the late 19th century."

He paused- for effect, I think. Everyone started clapping lightly and talking between themselves. Miss spinning ball started touching my baseball cap, smiling at me. She was becoming too much too fast. He began again in the same matter of fact way.

"It was Dutch Admiral Jacob Roggeveen who first sighted Easter Island on Easter day in 1722."

They really did have an in-house expert; I began to think. In addition, the spinning ball lady was kinda growing on me. I tried to listen as he went on.

"Most archeologist rely on dating the organic materials found at the Rano Ranaku quarry to ascertain a date of the stone figures. At best, they are no older then A.D.400."

I missed something in the translation. Nevertheless, everyone else began clapping one hand against the other. I hate when people do that. Perhaps I was paying closer attention to the spinning ball lady. For some reason Easter Island seemed a little fuzzy. I knew I had to get back on track so I did what anyone would do. I raised my hand.

"Gentleman in the third row, yes." He said looking directly at me.

This seemed a little odd considering there were only six of us standing there two people were in front of me, but I let it pass.

"How did we get from Jacob to 400 A.D." I asked, looking down at the spinning ball lady.

The question seemed reasonable to me but everyone else started staring at me like I was a complete idiot or I offended doctor peacock Hat-I wasn't sure which. I did the normal thing. I smiled at the spinning ball lady and shut up.

"My, are we the busybody, but I will backtrack for you mister no name."

I just smiled at the spinning ball lady.

"As I was saying, before someone interrupted me. Radiocarbon dating has placed the statues at around A.D. 400. The hard compressed volcanic Lapilli tuff was used to create the main bodies while a Red Scoria, which is another volcanic stone mind at Rano Ranaku, was used to produce the Topknots or cylindrical hats that are perfectly balanced on the heads of each figure."

Again he paused for effect; everyone did the stupid clap thing. I was impressed to say the least; doc peacock-feather really knew what he was talking about. Then again he could have been feeding a line of B.S. and I would've known the difference. I couldn't wait for what he was going to say next. It didn't take long.

"Besides the hundred or so Moai statues found on the outcropping, there are several other interesting artifacts such as the Basalt rock carving on the Island's southern tip, possibly used by, the birdman cult of the Island. I have several masks that depict this very interesting occult if anyone is interested; you'll find them over there somewhere."

We all looked towards where he was pointing. I wouldn't have known a Birdman cult mask from a Zulu warrior, but I looked anyway.

"These Petrography relief's can be traced back to ancient Egypt. A Crux Ansata was discovered carved in the back of one of the statues, that statue was removed and is on display in the British Museum. this alone proves beyond a shadow of doubt, a direct link between this Island and Mesopotamia by way of Egypt."

Again doctor peacock feather lost me, I started to raise my hand, but the spinning ball lady stopped me. She was starting to interest me more but the doc went on.

"There have been several attempts by some rather well educated persons in this field to explain how these statues were carved and erected, none of which are correct in my estimation. If we look at Thor Heyerdahl and that Czech engineer Paval

Pavel, whom I detest, they tried and failed miserably to walk a giant statue. We all know they weigh as much as 80 tons and are 30 feet in height. Impossible to walk a statue of that size. Made complete fools out of themselves. People, the Polynesians did not walk these statues in place, neither did they erect or carve them-simply a lie, lie, lie."

Doctor peacock-hat was really getting himself worked up. So was the spinning ball lady. I couldn't wait to hear what he had to say next.

"Those statues where ancient long before them island hopping Polynesians happened upon this outcropping around 1670.

To think that they could have carved them is ridiculous. The simple fact that these statues are to be found nowhere else in the Polynesian world has somehow slipped the minds of those trying to give credit for this magnificent carving feat to a group of people who still these things are their gods. It's not their fault but that Swiss Alfred Metraux who is to blame-and a couple other people as well."

"Who do you think built them Doc?" I tried to restrain myself, but I couldn't; it just came out. The spinning ball lady handed me back my hat. How she got it I am not sure, but she moved away just an inch or so.

Everyone else looked at me as if I had passed gas in an elevator. I felt kind of weak in the stomach, then again maybe I had passed gas and just didn't know it. I decided to shut up.

"Who built them you ask? The question should be why were they built Mr. No name?"

I wasn't going to bite.

"Before I tell you this" he said eyeing me. "Let me say this. If you have studied the features of the Moai Statues closely, then you would have seen that they bear a striking resemblance to peoples of the Mesopotamian area. The question is this why would a group of carvers carve the features of someone else, as opposed to their own?

Is it not reasonable to assume that if you are going to carve features on a statue you would at least carve the features of someone you knew-like yourself? Those statues are literally thousands of miles from Mesopotamia. Am I not right? And they're much closer to say South America. I see the light coming on. We are beginning to get it. The great mystery is coming clear."

I had no idea what he was talking about, but the spinning ball lady had my hat again and that was okay for now. I couldn't wait for him to continue.

"you see the closet relative carving to those on Easter Island can be found on the Olmec Heads at La Venta, Mexico where the carving depth and technique are quite the same. All one has to notice is the features of the Olmec heads and those features of the Olmec miner. What we see is the features of the African race. In particular those peoples of Equatorial Africa."

I found myself looking at a Zulu warrior mask and rubbing my head. I had no idea what direction he was going in, but I couldn't wait for him to continue.

"Those features of the Olmec are a direct link to the Kassite's of 2200 B.C. the ancient region of Elam where those very same miners where used to mine the Zagros Mountains for cassiterite, which is also found around Tiwanaku. This again is a direct link to Mesopotamia. Our Olmec are the same giants of Elam, and they built the statues on Easter Island."

Everyone again started that dumb clapping noise, but I couldn't restrain myself I came right out with it and said.

"How in the Hell did you come up with that doc?"

"There is no foul language allowed, Mr. No name."

"Sorry," I said but I wasn't going to let him off that easily. "You're trying to tell me doc that a group of Africans built those statues and some heads in Mexico. However, they didn't use their own faces, but the faces of someone else. Please you must think I am dumb as a box of rocks."

"Yes I am. And yes you are, and I can prove it."

"Know you can't prove none of that," I said

"Can to and I will." He said

"Prove it then, and I'd be careful if I were you doc. You can keep the hat if you want." I said to the spinning ball lady.

"What was that Mr. No name."

"I wasn't talking to you, moreover, what the dickens are cassiterite and a Tiwanaku?" I was getting a little worked up but I had to hear his proof.

"That would be Tin and Bolivia, Mr. No Name."

"I knew that."

"Did not." He shot back.

"Go on would you doc. I got three more just like that one at home."

"what did you say."

"I am not talking to you doc."

"Our friend people, wants to hear my proof. In that case let's not keep him waiting."

Everyone crowded in a little closer. Like I said before this was nothing like the unemployment line. I waited and it didn't take long.

"Easter Island was used as a penal colony for the Olmec who were the same people know as the Hamites of which Goliath was one? They were used to mine the Tin in Mexico and South America as well as Zagros Mountains in Mesopotamia.

"They became unruly and desecrated some water markers drawn out as massive figures on the plains of Nazca. And for this they were sentenced to Easter Island where they were ordered to build those huge statues with the features of their overseers on them. They were reprieved when their sentence was up, leaving some of the statues unfinished."

Again they all started with the clapping. I near the breaking point. There wasn't much more of this I could take, but the spinning ball lady seemed to be enjoying herself so I couldn't wait to hear what else the doc had to say and it didn't take him long. Nevertheless, before I let him go on. I had just one thing to say and I said it.

"Nobody in their right mind is going to believe that doc. That's the craziest thing I ever heard. Doc I'd like to know what happened to all those giants Africans. You can't hide a whole bucket full giants, now can you?"

I figured I had on the ropes now. So did the spinning ball lady. I could tell the way she leaned against me. It didn't take him long to recover. This is what he had to say: "They had their genetic code altered and were placed in Equatorial Africa. If you look closely at the Olmec heads you will see they look identical in every feature, except size, to the Pigmy, which is all the proof I need to conclude that the statues of Easter Island where carved by giant Pygmies before they were transmuted into little Pygmies."

I couldn't believe my ears but everyone else began clapping. The doc threw his peacock hat in the air. The purple hair lady started doing stretching exercises. To make matters worse, the spinning ball lady started rubbing my leg. I knew it was time for me to go. Moreover, I wanted my hat back I could take no more.

I smiled at the spinning ball lady, backed myself out towards the door. And made a beeline for my rambler. To my amazement Old faithful started on the first try. Even my Rambler had had about all it could take.

I figured once I got home I would phone my wife and tell her that she was right and I was wrong. Everything I ever said about Easter Island she would never hear again as long as I lived, and the phone company will never have to worry about my sister, sort of making calls to the physic hot line.

I drove on along the lake counting my blessing. I might share the same world as Doc peacock feather and the spinning ball lady; their slice just seemed a little more complicated than mine. On the other hand, mine probably seemed complicated to them. Doesn't make either of our points of view too strange, just different. After all, I paid them a visit and they paid a little bit of attention to me. Perhaps that's all any of us really want; just to be noticed if only for a short while. I drove on without a cre in the world.

My little slice of Cleveland began to look pretty good from my dirty windshield. Vermont and Mars belongs to someone else for the time being.

Tomorrow well that's a different day. I took a long pull from my warm Big Gulp. Popped in a David Allen Coe, and I really didn't care if my wife never calls me by my name.

# The End.

Spying on one's wife and her friends is a lot like spying on yourself well that's what happens in this funny story about love and marriage with the Big Red Hat Society thrown in for extra measure.

# Big Red Hat and All

I have always wondered what it would be like to spy on my wife. Don the whole espionage garb, fake beard, and mustache -- of course the KimYung Il, sunglasses. You see no good spy outfit would be complete without the sunglasses. Ever notice in all the great spy movies from the time of the immortal Charlie Chan to Hammer's Dick Barton special agent, Marlow's Sam Spade pure genius with a spy somewhere lurking in the back ground. Hollywood is simply clueless now with respect to making spy movies. I tell my wife this all the time; she just gives me a look and hides the TV guide. As I was saying, the first thing a spy puts on is his sunglasses. Does not matter if its 2am or high noon the glasses have to be on, which is somewhat ridiculous and of course a dead giveaway to who is the spy. But you wonder if he or she the spy, great actor Charlie Chan didn't care to much for the little hairy thingamajig at the bottom of his lip, never could figure out how to eat with chop sticks either.

Now that I have decided to spy on my wife, I am faced with a little bit of a dilemma; I do not really have a good reason to spy on her. You see after forty years of marriage one pretty much knows what the other half of their personality is up to. However, I still feel a need to seek out the underlying cause of what really goes on in that time void she has created, you know that grocery store abyss wives seem to fall head first into. It is a time void, a void of any time for me waiting at home for my snack. My wife has this strange ability to disappear for long periods at a time, by long I mean two hours at tops, nevertheless at sixty-nine two hours is an eternity and not to mention three quarters of football with a nap thrown in for good measure.

    She seems to enjoy taking off on those little escapades' of hers right after those magic words. You know the catch phrase we husbands look for, our mental note to get ready for Armageddon, or meat loaf. Mary's that is my wife by the way, her catch phrase is, "Dear I'll be back in five minutes, we need milk". I know it is a rather long catch-phrase-by-catch-phrase standard; however its effective and two hours later she'll return with a two week supply of goat cheese and no milk. Reason to spy, I will let you decide.

    I've given some thought too, and did the mathematics on how it is nearly impossible to spend two hours shopping for milk, to come back with more goat cheese than Madelyn Miller the TravelLady eats in a year and I'm told she eats a lot of goat cheese, lives off the stuff,.

It just does not add up perhaps I should spy on Madelyn, or the people that make goat cheese.

      Spying on one's wife seems to be one of those things men naturally think about, not that I spend a great deal of time thinking about my wife, I do not. However, when I do its only instinctive to wonder what she is up to, like breathing. Strange how the mind works, one minute you are completely thoughtless, the next minute you got an itch you cannot reach.

      It is only expected to be concerned about one's spouse, which is just how my mind works. Men do not have to put a great deal of thought into solving simple tasks the solution comes instinctively to us. My wife on the other hand agrees to disagree with my last statement. She is always asking me in a kind of pointed manner why I leave the toilet seat up. To her it is a simple matter of putting the seat back down, in my defense, I have explained to her; by leaving, the seat up it frees my mind of unnecessary contemplation so I can concentrate on more pressing things at hand. Like an emergency dash to the john.

Forty seconds is about as long as a time out last in football and you never know what commercials you have not seen. I have to get in and get out, man logic I point out to her.

I have explained my logical approach to solving two problems at once; I do not think she gets it. Hard to figure she just shakes her head at me and says. "I'll be back dear in five minutes we need milk." Two hours later well you guessed it damn goat cheese.

It appears that when I have the most time to contemplate spying on my wife, comes in what I call my hazy zone. That period one's mind goes from babbling to itself to not hearing someone else babbling at you. It is in that babbling to myself period when I visualize spying on my wife.

Like most retired couples living out there last remaining days, between too many Parcheesi nights and fighting over the last bowl of Jell-O. We do try to live a modestly quiet life; well at least we did once upon a blue moon when we called the Windy City home. Now all bets are off on the quite part of self-seclusion.

You'd think that now that our children are grown and married, riding their own personal wave of self-indulgence, forgetting about our contribution of eighteen plus years of agreeing with all the particulars that come with parenthood they visit more often than they do, and call at a descent hour. David our oldest was properly married that is by rabbi Goldstienburger, good man cannot understand a word he says but good man at any rate. On the other hand, Emily our daughter has decided that tradition has nothing to do with her modern way of thinking, I think she needs a traditional kick in...love does traditionally look the other way when it is your children upsetting the natural progression of things.

Happy Haven, I hate it here to pretenses for me, on the other hand, Mary Ellen is like a 67-year-old grandma in a fabric store, were everything is half off and you get a free Thimbu that serves no propose with every purchase. Life is just one big patchwork quilt to her, held together by hope and poligrip, I really do hate it here, but love does look the other way when your wife's happiness is at stake.

Six months ago, we moved to Happy Haven, retirement community here in Orlando Florida. Seemed like a good idea after forty plus years of knee-deep snow and two bunions the size of Eddy Fishers last divorce settlement. It was time to leave all those old memories and busy body neighbors behind, I like to talk about the good old days of repressive memories, my wife thinks the past means past.. Reminiscing about unconstrained comfort, a total fabrication of the thought process I might add. Were for some reason freezing your matzo balls off for just for the satisfaction of living in a place where your parents ended up to broke to leave and to stubborn to want to leave even if they could. Yes the good old days of melancholy thoughts that takes you back to when your mother's home baked bread tasted like a memory of pure happiness. I've simply over looked the fact my father had us say grace after we ate, never got the humor in that as a child but now as I look back, it was funny the look on my mother's face, he would always kiss her forehead and laugh holding his favorite part of her bread the end of the loaf.

    Like most retired people, we try to live a quiet life, well at least I have tried, and my wife on the other hand has managed to make friends with everyone from the mail carrier to the battery sells men for the electric scooters that seem to be everywhere. What is with that, I wonder as soon as you reach 70 what you forget how to walk. I cannot walk five feet out my door without some near sighted old geezer zipping by me at a 10 miles an hour, horn blasting and tope blowing in the wind, unnerving is what it is. In the last six months, we have been to eight weddings, ten funerals and two bris, poor little follows. After the last bris I had, had enough I told Mary Ellen stop making friends and get a cat, no cat yet but next Saturday another brisk poor little follow.

For a while, there life was good, a little peace and quiet had fallen on Happy Haven. My wife had given up the idea of entertaining everyone in town. Moreover, everyone in town had given up the idea of being entertained by my wife, a fair trade off as far as I was concerned. Nevertheless, all good things gotta come to an end, like the last piece of

German chocolate cake that some saddest decided to cut the top off, instead of taking a normal piece like a normal person. What kind of person would do that, just venting. As I was saying, all good things and German chocolate cake gotta come to an end.

    One lazy uneventful Saturday afternoon, I was lounging around in my lazy boy, thinking about mowing the lawn. You know sizing up the task at hand. Milling over the best way to tackle the daunting job. I was startled awake, shocked into disbelief, dumbfounded by a multicolored form hovering before. It seemed my wife had donned a huge, I mean really huge red hat, with chicken feathers, maybe parrot plumes coming out of the top and sides of it. Do parrots have plumes? not sure but it was huge. The hat that is, not the plumage, at any rate, besides the La Cage Le Folly hat she was wearing. She also had on a god awful looking purple dress. My wife looked like a crazed menopausal flapper, with a Betty Boop complex, granted a sixty seven year old Jewish grandmother version of Betty Boop without the Boop.

What can I say about the dress it was purple? First thing, that came to my mind was what kind of person wears a purple dress. I had totally forgotten about mowing the lawn, and the German chocolate cake at Mort Steimiers funeral three weeks ago was completely set aside I had bigger fish to fry.

"What do you think Oscar?"

How does one respond to such a question without sounding rude? I thought for a moment, the idea of being nice entered my mind only for a second.

"What do I think? You scar me half to death grinning at me dressed like a dysfunctional Mary Poppins with an umppa luppa complex, and you ask me what I think".

"I think you've finely lost your mind Mary Ellen Finderhouse, you really need a new fashion consultant or a cat".

"Don't be ridicules Oscar, lost my mind indeed and what is an umppa luppa complex, are you saying I'm short and fat, Oscar is that what you think".

"Your purple, Mary Ellen with a big red hat, with chicken feathers coming out of it you look like Willy Wonkas house keeper".

"There you go again with the insults Oscar, I look great, I feel great, get use to it you old, old fart! Why do I bother with you Oscar".

I was not sure what to say, Mary Ellen, seems she had the last word. The old fart, pretty much summed up the whole ordeal, well at least from her point of view. Yes indeed she was a little on the frazzled side, I would have to keep a close eye on her, there was something afoot here and I had to get to the bottom of this extreme makeover, after my nap that is.

"Oscar before you completely ignore me with your second nap of the day, I need to tell you something dear."

"And what might that be".

"I joined a society".

"You can't join a society your apart of society, that's like saying I changed my sex how much sense does that make Mary Ellen, I joined a society my foot".

"Well I did, and would you like for me to call the Mohel".

"That's just rich Mary Ellen; perhaps I should call the fashion police".

Things were looking a little blink at the moment, I wasn't sure what was coming next, Mary Ellen was looking at me from beneath her big red hat brim with a strange grin on her face. After forty years of marriage you think you know someone this was a whole new twist not sure, how I should digest this I joined a society statement. I needed a sandwich, more importantly I needed to go look out the front window to make sure there wasn't a yellow brick road outside my house, had there been a tornado while I was napping I thought..

"Mary Ellen".

"Yes dear".

"Was there a tornado today"?

"Tornado Oscar why would you ask me that of course there wasn't a tornado what's wrong with you"?

"Just checking".

Yes, I needed a sandwich and a pair of Kim Yung Il sunglasses.

"Were did you get the hat dear"?

"Don't play coy with me Oscar I know when you're up to something and why would you ask if there was a tornado Oscar I just don't get you sometimes, would you like a sandwich dear".

"Good lord, you come home looking like I don't know what without Toe doo I might add, I ask you were you got that hat didn't bring up the dress by the way and you think I'm up to something, well I'm not and yes I would no damn goat cheese on it please".

"Watch your language Oscar, you always have cheese on your sandwich now you don't want any are you okay dear".

"I'm fine".

"Oscar I'm the new Queen mom of the Happy Haven, Fleur- de-leis, blue birds. I joined the Big Red Hat society are you excited for me Oscar".

"I'm beside myself dear, I have no idea what you just said, did you join an occult Mary Ellen? You see this is just the reason why I wanted to stay in Chicago, people move down here and start driving around in golf carts and electric wheel chairs and joining Occults like it's the thing to do, I'll have none of this nonsense, what's next canary sacrifices, do the neighbors need to hide their pets from us now".

"I'm going to ignore all that Oscar, and make you a sandwich, the girls will be here in an hour dear, so no more napping I thought you were going to mow the lawn today it won't mow its self".

All I could do was look at Mary Ellen, time for a bathroom dash, not that I had to go I just needed a moment to sort things out, get my plan in order not sure yet what I would do there was just too much going on right now. I thought as I walked towards the bathroom door who were these girls, I was sure they were not dancing girls, thought about that, a house full of geriatric dancing girls not sure I could take it or if it was even legal. Turning on the water pretty much forced the issue. I really did have to go, listening at the door for some tall sign of what was coming next, nothing just silence. A kind of spooky silence only a paranoid husband could imagine. Was that it, had this uncanny fashion show made me paranoid, if so what was I paranoid about? Flushing I decided to face that paranoia head on.

The whole aspect of spying on my wife now had a completely new meaning; I would foil this evil plan and have a bowl of lentil soup. I needed the perfect plan, I needed more crackers in my soup, I needed another nap but most of all I needed to call my uncle Sid in Poland, New Jersey he had spied on his wife once ended in a disaster but he knew the business.

"Dear is Sid still alive".

"Who Cid Caesar, if he is Oscar it would be a miracle. Drank too much and those woman. I once heard".

"Not Cid Caesar for Pete sake, will you listen, my uncle Cid in Poland".

"He died in 1966, Oscar the same year we were married. Drank himself to death ".

"He was hit by a Bus now that I remember, he never drank".

"Oscar he walked in front of a Bus drunk".

"Not the same thing".

"Why Oscar thinking about calling him, maybe a little visit?"

I ignored Mary Ellen it was becoming pretty easy today to ignore her, it was time for me to put my master plan in action, I didn't need Cid's advice and his wife drove him to drink now that I thought about it, I would wing it, I've seen enough spy movies I knew the business inside and out.

"Dear I need to go and get some gas and oil for the mower I'll be back in an hour or so enjoy your company".

"It's electric Oscar".

"What's Electric".

"The Lawn mower Oscar It's electric".

Damn I thought foiled already, how does she know these things. Had to think quick.

"I know that dear. I was just testing you, see if you knew that."

"Have fun dear and say hi to Marge for me she's watering her lawn".

" Damn I thought now I would have to talk to Phil and his busy body wife, things were getting out of hand my plan was in jeopardy I had to think damn Phil and Marge and she still has that hat on.

"Will be having a blue bird meeting when you get back please be nice, Oscar for me"

"What in the devil is a blue bird meeting did I miss something."

"My society Oscar you never listen to a word I say".

"That's another thing what the dickens is this society thing, are you a red hat wearing communist Mary Ellen. I will have no part of the Communist party, remember Mort Bleakenmen. He couldn't sake that label for years and all he did was put a bumper sticker of Lenin voting for Ford on his Lincoln it was a joke, but no, good old Mort paid dearly for that, couldn't get anyone to service his car or sell him marble rye. Is that what you want Mary Ellen".

"Are you done Oscar?"

"What nothing to say about that you know I like marble rye."

"Have fun Oscar I'll see you in a little while."

Things were beginning to make less sense as I weighed my options. My wife said she was the queen mom of, what did she say. Fleur-de-lis, blue birds. I will have to do some research on these fleurs-de-lis; it sounds French, wonder if there is any French communist living in Happy Haven. She let slip the name of this secret society. The Red Hat Society, what is with the purple dress, a rouge to throw me off their trail? Moreover, they will all be flocking together these blue birds from France at my house this afternoon, how convenient. I had work to do and not a minute to waste. Happy Haven was beginning to look a little less happy, well at least on Bridgemore Drive, at any rate.

I spent a little more time then I intended in the costume store. Amazing how many different disguises there are. A whole cottage industry could be created around spying on ones wife, and the people were very helpful, merchandise. Finally I found the perfect pair of Kim Yong Il sunglasses the Hermit dictator would be impressed with these knock off from I'm sure his personal collection. In addition, the bread well it was a little too long it highlighted my hair well, at least that is what the nice sells woman said, highlighted my hair. Mary Ellen never said anything like that before. After an hour, I knew it was time to leave this oasis of espionage behind. I felt sad in a spying kind of way. Nevertheless those Blue Birds from France were about to descend on my house and there was work to be done but first I needed a Fresca and a slice of marble rye, I was off to Phil's Deli on ninth and main.

  I counted 10, maybe there were 13, Red Hatters not sure my glasses fell off when one of the ladies bent down to pick up her hat. Make a note keep an eye on the big blonde-haired woman.

The hedge between my house and Phil's garage made a perfect area for my sting operation. I could see them talking away in the living room, sipping tea. The big blonde-haired woman was eating a cookie, one of my Oreo's "make a note, get more Oreo's"

Mary Ellen, seemed so happy smiling sharing my cookies with everyone of her knew friends. They were laughing really enjoying themselves. I watched them as they gathered around the kitchen table, like so many woman do, comparing a recipe or idea or simply an antidote about a man they noticed in a whimsical discrete manner. maybe I was there an half hour maybe not quite that long it didn't matter just kneeing behind Phil's hedge wandering with curious invasion of what was going on in my home , the silent contemplation seemed to remove me from what my mission was all about. Phil's garage door opened with a whining jerking noise rousing me from my haphazard stoop. A close call even for the highest trained in the area of espionage, I being mid-grade seeing that this being my first real case , back tracking more to the effect of standing coughing and moving on but slough like at any rate.

Slipping into my own yard was easy compared to the ordeal of Phil's garage door nearly had a heart attack nevertheless I made it through the breech. I placed my disguise under the lawn mower, careful not to scratch my Kim Yong Il sunglasses, rubbing my chin too rid it of any tall tale signs of my intentions. I made my way completely secure of my success towards my back door, breathing I entered clearing my throat for effect.

"Oscar is that you dear".

"Know its Liberaracce; I'm here to get my hat back".

"Stop it Oscar, come in and meet the girls, ladies this is my husband Oscar."

" Pleasure all mine ladies, being your queen mom husband whatever, I think you all look wonderful in your hats and dresses and society stuff, so with that I think I'll have an Oreo cookie and get out of your way, ladies I bid you ado."

"Oscar will be done in a little bit and well don't get to comfortable ado."

"Take your time my dear; we might need more cookies by the way."

"He seems such a nice man, Mary Ellen how long have you been married,"

I watched the exchange between my wife and Blondie from the uneasy comfort of my Lazy Boy, trying not to make eye contact with Mary Ellen-harder than it seemed since she was watching me watch her, kind of unnerving to be honest, but I held my ground and last cookie.

I could hear them laughing, talking about how Neil Diamond was better looking than Tom Jones, thought about that and voted for Tom Jones, the whole wanna see me do my thing pull my chain made more since then Mandy. She was happy in a kind of way I had not seen in a long time. I just sat back and blocked out the chatter and running water from my kitchen. Slipping into a fog of lost memories, tied by a male bound of selective reasoning that ask with convection why in the hell Hogan never just left Stalag 13 was Klink that stupid, when I felt Mary Ellen touching my arm, I looked up at her, hat gone smiling at me.

    After forty years of marriage, not much comes by way of surprise. It is that predictability we husbands depend on to make sure the cart is heading in the right direction, granted we assume we are driving that preverbal cart. However, trying to understand the female mind is a task better left for the female mind. My wife has a tendency to tell me to put myself in her shoes when I state the obvious to her, of course what is obvious to me is not obvious to her how is that I often wondered.

For over a month now I have perfected the art of spying, I learned rather quickly when spying on one's wife when she is with a group of purple dress big red hat wearing ladies, you are in fact spying on the whole kick and caboodle, everyone becomes suspect in this game of cat and mouse.

I have become a multi-tasking spy and my wife said I could never do more than one thing at a time. How wrong she was once again I have out witted her. Following Mary Ellen, and her troupe of multicolored hats, through the geriatric streets of Happy Haven was indeed a task. Trying to avoid the onslaught of electric wheel chairs and golf carts was the hardest part of my life as a spy. Amazing how many people, you know that walk around at night well between the hours of eight and nine at tops drive around in an assistant vehicle during the day. I asked one gentleman holding a paper close to my mouth, to disguise my voice what he called the contraption he was driving "assistant vehicle" he said and what in the hell is wrong with that bread he added, I left on that note. I knew who he was but he did not know who I was, positive he was the one that mutilated the German chocolate cake; I said nothing moving on hastily watching him watch me.

Yes, Mary Ellen seemed happy, and I felt unsure like an Island in a stream that flows backwards into the memories of one's mind. All those memories that seem to matter only after you have seen yourself in the eyes of someone you love. It is a fine line, I know between love and marriage, but I understand that line well. What I have trouble with is this need to spy on Mary Ellen and her new friends.

Mary Ellen has in some strange way become younger a strange transformation has fallen over my wife these last few months. It is nearly impossible to explain but in some way I am happy for her, I have grown close to watching her friends with a curious interest of admiration.

The highlight of my week is when the women all get together to plan their outings. It affords me the needed mental exercise to consult all my spying skills, you know compiling a well-planned assault on a bunch of old ladies unsuspecting absent mindedness like taking pudding from ninety year old, how sweet it is to be one step ahead of one's wife and her troupe.

So far my operation has been off the fly, I like it that way improvising as I go along. Strange thing so far I noticed that none of the places they have visited have had any National Security value or any value at all. Nevertheless this game of cat and mouse has made life in Happy Haven, interesting I would not go so far as say happy, at sixty-nine content is much better than happy in my book.

As I followed my wife and her entourage into a teahouse Saturday afternoon, in what Happy Havenites call the better part of town, which of course makes no sense because every part of town looks the same. My undercover operation was almost foiled when my beard fell off and into my cup of Earl Gray Breakfast blend; two busy body red hatters started staring at me as if I was Beelzebub himself, narrow escape. Make a note; never drink your Earl Gray once a fake beard falls in it.

Yes spying on one's wife can be a trying ordeal, but yet it is amazing how much in common you have with your spouse. We often times take each other for granted in our everyday appeal at normalcy. I have learned a great deal about The Happy Haven, Red Hat Society, Blue Bird, purple dress wearing grandmas. Their no threat to the common good or social fabric of this nation the French connection is still up for debate but be that as it may, I just simply needed an excuse to be a part of something that didn't include me.

Us men have our own little clubs, Elks, Great Water Buffalo were we look up to our Grand Po Ba, and contemplate the mysteries of our wives mind and why they built an over pass over Market street. Greater things of life and who died lately but it all seems different when our wives have found shelter or friendship in a mutual company of their choosing.

I Love Mary Ellen, I know I have a strange way of showing it, but sometimes you have to take the high road to get back on the low road your mind has allowed you to travel along, a destination defined by years of thinking that somehow you know more than what life has taught you.

Mary Ellen does at times need a different kind happiness, than the same emotional hayride supplied by an old man. That adjusts his weighted clock of habit to read the same hour, rather than the habit of time adjusting the old man to see his wife as not clockwork, but a person that only wants to express herself as she sees fit without fear, without pressure but with love.

I'm proud of my wife, and I do admire her knew found friends, now that I have seen their little piece of happiness through the haze of my own discontent. Mary Ellen slips into the house now quite but always with a smile after her meetings, biscuits, and tea. Somehow I believes she knows that it was me behind the fake beard and heavy sunglasses, peaking at her and her friends from behind my warn Saturday Evening Post. However, I am to cagy for her and those Blue Birds, nevertheless I think she knows.

"Oscar"

"Yes dear"

"I picked up a little something for you, when I went out for milk."

"Let me guess goat cheese."

"Don't be silly Oscar it's on the bed."

I watched Mary Ellen for a minute I was not sure what she was up to. I wasn't sure if I wanted to go into the bed room and find out what she had got me. In lazy indifference and shuffling feet, I made my way into the bedroom looking over my shoulder to see if she was watching me pretend it did not matter. Mary Ellen busied herself ignoring me over a pot of black beans.

There they were in all their glory just lying there on the bed; I couldn't help but laugh out loud, as I eased myself down on the bed to try them on. The fake beard was shorter than the one I had and the Kim Yung Il glasses were perfect, I looked in the old chipped mirror above the dresser and yes the beard highlighted my faded gray hair just right.

Perhaps I had joined my own secret society, a society where a man finds himself by way of spying on his wife. I do not spy on Mary Ellen and her friends anymore, there no need, Bridgemore Drive is safe and sound these days, with the Red Hat Society doing all they can to keep an old man safe and happy. I just wish they did something about those god-awful purple dresses.

"Oscar we need milk I'll be back in five minutes."

"Here we go again."

The End

EUGENE WILLIAMS

Plum Loco

Complete story from "Uncommon Notions" Story about a wayward Cowboy fired from the railroad and ends up in a mining town where he gets some bad news and a lesson from a Chinaman deputy. Pike North is really in for it and so is the Town of Mud Flats when he gets there...

Two Days before the hanging:

    I hadn't finished moving my shavin' razor from my right cheek to my left, before I done killed two Chinamen out right. Daggone Chinamen more trouble than a pack of Paddies pounding rail at four in the morning. Gotta hand it to those coolies, they sure are a working bunch of little fellas ever there been. Shame, how I hadda kill'em every now and again. Never-you mind any apologies from me, over why I am here today, mind you Doc.

I can't say I feel bad about killin darn near everyone in Mud Flats. If ever a town needed killen Mud Flats was it. Here comes that dang blasted Hangman agin. He keeps just walking by me, grinning. Back and forth, back and forth. Dangeest thing I ever saw.

Why there's a Hanging' in the first place:

Now I reckon Big Boss man, you're probably wondering why I had to kill those two fellas outright. Didn't give me much choice in the matter, no sir they didn't. I was dipping my straight razor into this here bucket of water the Chinaman over yonder was holding. Fella was shaking so dang blasted much, I nearly cut my own throat. Water pouring over the sides of the bucket like a bath barrel shot full of holes. Got my new boots plum soaked.

I figured I help the fella stop shaking by shooting him in the gullet. I did on both accounts. When I turned back towards my looking tin, there was another Chinaman running to beat all get out, with my looking tin. I had no choice but to killem right on the spot.

I know before you go on, it being illegal to shoot a Chinaman, but this one had my tin looking glass. By gum, that made it real legal like. Now the first one well, Big Boss man, he fell in the gray area of sorts. I'll tell ya this much, when I let loose on the little fella with my lookin' tin, he let out a yell, then rolled over and died right out. Don't take much to kill a Chinaman. That's pretty much how it happened, Big Boss man.

Sorry about killin the shaky one, but the other had it comen.

"Well Pike," Big Boss man said, eyeing me real good. He took a big yank off his plug of tobakey. Wallowed it around in his hog jaws, went to spit out a wad of juice like he does. Dang gone whole affair shot out his mouth about a pinky finger distance, fell plum on his belly. I just looked him over, knew better than to say anything; he was already fit to be tied over the two Chinamen. I just waited until he wiped himself with his sleeve and yanked off another chew.

"Well Pike, I just can't figure it. I've been laying track fur the Union-Pacific since the first spike driven at Omaha. You been with me now a little over three weeks only on account I known your daddy.

Good man, sorry about the whole affair in Ogden, but, well Pike, he kinda had it coming, Preacher wife and all dang Mormons. I am sure if your daddy would have known it was his wife."

I had to interrupe Big Boss man even though he doesn't cotton to anyone breaking his wording none.

"Dang Blasted, Big Boss man preacher had five wives."

" Now Pike, I was a talkin', all the same your daddy he was a good man. Now, Pike, in the three weeks you've been working fur me, you've managed to kill sixteen Chinamen, fur various reasons no less, some questionable like this one here. Well, Pike, some I granted legal like that one there."

Big Boss man didn't give me much choice again. I had to sit him straight, on account he had the Chinaman confused. I said. "It was this one here legal. And that one there, questionable, Big Boss man."

"Well, Pike, I was a talkin', can't tell this on from that one no how, but whichever the case may be. Well Pike theres been a whole pickle barrel of talk about you lately. Some are of the opinion that you don't like China-men much, granted this opinion is unanimous among the Chinamen.

" Well, Pike, if there had only been two, maybe four, killed outright I might be inclined to think perhaps your being unfairly judged. I knew your daddy and he seemed get along just fine with the Chinaman."

Big Boss man was heading in the wrong direction as far as I was concerned. I had to put my two cents in. I said. "I aint got nothin' agin no Chinamen Big Boss man."

"Well, Pike, I was a talkin'. I figured you leave me with little choice but to let you go Pike. Besides at the rate you're going there won't be any chinamen left in the world outside of a year if I kelp you on. I can't do that now Pike, railroad needs Chinamen. I knew your daddy and he see it my way. You got five minutes Pike to get your things together and skidaddle. I gotta turn this matter over to the Railroad, but don't worry, these two aren't gonna tell on ya. Been nice working with ya Pike."

"If that don't beat all." I said walking away from Big Boss man. He just plum came out and gave me the boot, ain't never been kicked off no job. I was hotter than a pepper-sprout, by gum.

Big Boss man wasn't someone you killed very easy and I wasn't about to killem over no Chinaman. I figured I just saddle up my horse and high tail it towards Caliornye. Didn't rightfully know what I was gonna do fur work. Maybe bust some broncos or herd some cattle, I'd play by ear.

It was getting along late in the year when I happened upon a mining town called Silver Dog in the high Sierras. Place had seen better days but so had I, been riding going-on two weeks and my belly was plum empty.

I figured I'd head into the saloon and wash the dust out my gums and the hunger out of my belly, maybe get in a hand or two of Black Jack. I step on up to the bar, and said.

"Whiskey bar keep."

"What's your name fella?"

"Doggonna, a man gotta tell ya his name before he can get a whiskey?" I said I was tired and fit to be tied over getting kicked off the job, ain't never been kicked off a job. The last thing I wanted was a parley with a bar keep.

"Nope, just trying make social mister," he said.

"I don't feel social mister, how about that whiskey?" I said.

That dang blasted talky talk bar keep handed me a half-cooked bottle of old number 9 and I fell into a chair, kicked my feet upon the table, and went to work on my dust and belly.

I made good of about two fingers when I noticed a dapper dressed fella giving me the eye over his playing hand. Looking at me unnoticed like but I noticed him looking and fiddling with his hand, being it's not polite to look at a fella while he's curing himself from a long ride, I got plum set on fire right quickly. I started to pull myself away from the table, when the dapper fella throws his hand down and got up and headed my way.

Being I was in a strange town, natural thing to do was to slide my right hand onto my hog leg, and pull back the hammer. I waited snake like to see what was on his mind. I gave the place the once over. The piano man was plucking away and everyone else was as cool as cucumbers. I just couldn't figure this dapper fella for a troublemaker, didn't have that look- beady eyes or knife scar running down the side of his face. Nope this fella was prim and proper. Lady like, it didn't matter much no how I was gonna give him all the trouble and then some as soon as he got another foot closer.

He must have seen I was business like on account he stopped dead in his tracks, about four arms from me. The piano man knew something was cooking.

They always do. He stopped plucking, and everyone turned my way. Now I have been in a many a saloon ruckus, so I played my hand by eyeing everyone and no one in particular. Then the dapper fella said, "You must be Pike North. Mind if I pull up a chair and join you."

Now when a fella in a town you have never been in knows who you are, then that can't mean anything good, but this dapper fella had my full attention, so I was obliged to say. "Well mister, you got me at an advantage, and I don't cotton to strangers knowing me fur I know them. All things being equal, I'll lend you an ear. Just mind your time right smartly, wouldn't want to fill those fancy duds with holes now."

"Dangest way of saying sit down I ever heard Pike," he said, smiling at me all friendly like. "Don't mind if I call you Pike now do ya."

I could tell this fella wasn't lookin' to get killed outright. You can always tell when a fella trying to get himself killed. He does and that ends that. I nodded to the fella.

"I reckon since you already know who I am no sense in changing this here horse in mid-stream, I said.

"Reckon your right Pike," he said. Then he went on into a parley of sorts. "By the way my name is Tennessee Bill. My friends call me Dr. Bill on account I used to be a barber in Tennessee that is."

"Figures about right, Dr. Bill pleasure, to meet ya," I said.

I extended my hand friendly like. This fella seemed fine by me, being from Tennessee explained his dudes out right and a doctor and all. I never known no back shooting Tennessee doctor, so I slid my hand off my Colt 44, tried to relax a bit. Now being in a strange town chopping away on the bit with a Tennessee doc didn't help matters.

"I hope you don't mind me asking how you'd come about the handle Pike?" he said.

"My daddy named me after a fish, but I wouldn't go spreading that around now Dr. Bill," I said.

I slid my hand back on my hog leg so he gets my meaning real good. He did and that was that for the time being.

I offered Dr. Bill a pull from my Red eye. He declined. Said fella was gonna need some dental work later on, seemed he had to have his wits about him. I reckon being a doctor and all I wouldn't force the issue. Under normal terms, I would have been taken back by a fella not tossing back a shot or two with me, but being a doctor and all I let it go.

"I knowed your Daddy, Pike," he said, smiling at me all friendly like. Seems lately a lot of fella's known my daddy I thought, but I let it pass. He went on. "Good man, sorry about what happen, but he had it coming."

"Well Dr. Bill he didn't know the Preacher was married. Dang blasted Mormons," I said tossing back another shot, eyeing ole Dr. Bill real careful like.

"Yep I reckon Pike." He said. " I hate to be the bearer of bad news, but there's been some trouble in Mud Flats. I can't get into it. That's for the sheriff to go over with ya. Everyone this side of the Continental Divide been looking for ya Pike. I known your daddy. So I kinda knowed you, of sorts.

"Being there ain't no other Pike North that got every Chinaman this side of Chinaman land fit to be tied at him, so as soon as I heard a stranger was in town that got booted off the railroad, I figured."

"You sure have done a lot of figuring, haven't ya Dr. Bill?" I said. I was getting mighty tired of Dr. Bill parleying with his fancy words and dudes and all, but I wasn't fit to be tied yet.

So I said. "You figured right, but I wouldn't be bringing up the railroad now Dr. Bill; that's a sore spot and it ain't gonna heal anytime soon. Let's just stick to higher ground as far as the Chinamen; I ain't got nothing' to say on that subject. What kind of trouble you'd be talking about Dr. Bill?"

Old Dr. Bill figured he may have said a bit much. I could see he was nervy like in his chair. I let him squirm about, eyeing him real good.

"Like I said Pike that's for the sheriff to feel you in on. Name's Lawson, Frank Lawson. Ever heard of him Pike?"

"Yep, I heard of him," I said. "And that dang blasted deputy of his. Both of them two sidewinders use to work for the railroad. Yep I heard of Lawson, Frank Lawson."

I had to take another swallow of my red eye, calm my nerves a bit.

"Well, Pike, I gotta get on, I'll be over at the Barber waitin' for my docterin; fella gonna need some work done on him the way I figure it."

I kept my eye on Dr. Bill; something just didn't set right. I couldn't put my finger on it. He seemed to know too much about me, and that never is a good sign, being in a strange town and all.

I tossed back another shot and tossed four bits at the Keep. No sense in playing nice, since everyone knew who I was.

Lawson, Frank Lawson it was time for me to find out what was airing and I didn't take kindly to bad news.

I headed straight for the jailhouse, adjusted my hog leg low, butt out so I could cross draw on any man with the a mind to get himself killed outright.

I pulled my Bowie out, wiped the blade across my left chap leg, slid it back in its keep. Low on my right calve like. Comes in handy there when fighting on the ground, can stick a man clean through the gullet before he has a mind to know what happened.

I walked up on the jail porch, took a look around; there wasn't a soul in sight. I had a bad feeling about Lawson, Frank Lawson, but ole Dr. Bill said he needed to see me about some bad news and I don't cotton to no bad news.

I griped my hog leg, pushed in the jailhouse door with the toe of my boot, and walked in slow like. Lawson, Frank Lawson was standing by the potbelly stove with his back to me, his no account Deputy was glaring at me as I walked in snake like.

Lawson, Frank Lawson, turned on his heels, set down the his broken off handle coffee mug, and yelled to beat the devil. "Get um Kim Lee!"

Now you're not ever quite prepared for a four-foot-tall Chinaman deputy doing a back flip straight up in the air and landing on his haunches dead center of a writing table a foot in front of you.

Before I could cross draw on the polecat, he kicked me dead center in my mouth, sending both my front teeth into my belly. I nearly flew right back out the door. I steadied myself and ran in for the charge.

The little polecat leaped over my head as I crashed into the writing table busting the dang blasted thing into a hundred pieces.

I went for my Bowie, figured he'd jump on me like a bronco while I was down. He did, climbing around my neck, chopping me on top of the head and the side of my neck. Like there was no tomorrow.

I got a good hold of him around the pigtail and threw the little fella smack dab into the potbelly stove. He let out a scream, did another flippin' thingamajig, and kicked me straight in the gullet, so dang blasted hard that both my hands went numb.

I couldn't feel my doggone fingers. The little polecat charged in on me headfirst and started ripping away on my belly with his teeth. Only thing I could do was try and hack him to death with my forearms.

I finally got him lifted up high enough so I could knee him straight in the family jewels, he rolled over, began hollering but still full of fight.

I tried like the dickens to hold him down so I could get my colt out with my forearms which is dang near impossible. I figured I could brace the barrel against his head and slip my boot off and pull the trigger with my big toe. He wasn't having none of that. Somehow he broke lose, and did another one of those flipping things and kicked me clean out the window.

I landed straight on my back in the middle of the horse trough. My whole dang blasted mouth was pouring out blood from my missing two front teeth and my hands were still full asleep.

I tried like the wind to pull myself out of the trough. When I looked up this crazy little Chinaman was standing on the jail house porch with a double barrel shot gun leveled clean on me.

I drove under the water and tried to plaster myself to the bottom of the trough. He let loose both barrels.

Water started draining out the blasted thing and I knew the next one would do me in. I stuck my bootless foot out the trough full well expecting to see my leg go flying by. But it was as quite as a horse funeral.

I stuck my head up and Kim Lee was laid out on the porch, with sheriff Lawson, Frank Lawson, standing their holding a hickory club grinning at me. I didn't know what to make of the whole affair but I was fit to be tied.

"You can come out now, Pike," he said

My hands began to work and I wanted to kill that little Chinaman before he woke, but the sheriff wasn't having none of that. I charged the little polecat. I lifted up my foot. I planned on stomping him to death. Before I knowed what hit me that dang blasted Lawson, Frank Lawson, whacked me a good one across my belly. Knocked what wind I had in me clean out, to make matters worse he took my colt and Bowie.

"Now, Pike, we were only having some fun with ya," he said.

I tossed up my two front teeth right there on the porch and wanted to kill them two polecat lawmen dead as ever. I couldn't see the humor in this, but I was beat to pieces, so I sat down beside the sleeping Chinaman and stared at Lawson, Frank Lawson and shook my head.

"Sorry about that Pike," he said. "But you had it comin'. Kim Lee's been waiting to beat the tar out of you for months now. I wouldn't be wanting to do anything about this if I were you Pike; Kim Lee is a lawman at any rate."

"Lawman or not," I said. "I am gonna kill him as soon as I dry off and I might kill you for good measure."

"Now Pike, we were only funnin' you Dr. Bill will fix your teeth fur ya," he said handing me back my colt and Bowie. "Don't do nothing you'll regret." He said, smacking that dang blasted hickory club in his hand.

I knew this was one of them double crossing plans now. That no account Dr. Bill was in on this all along. I was gonna kill him good as soon as he fixed my teeth.

"I know you Pike," Sheriff Lawson, Frank Lawson said. "I know what you're thinking. Dr. Bill stopped by, told us you were in town. He didn't have nothin' to do with Kim Lee here going plum loco on you."

"He sure knew someone was gonna get his teeth fixed and that's all the proof I need," I said back wiping my mouth on my sleeve.

"Everybody in Silver Dog needs their teeth fixed Pike. But I got some bad news fur ya," he said.

"Well out with it sheriff," I said, picking up my two teeth off Kim Lee's chest where they flew out to. I wiped them on Kim Lee's shirt and put um in my upper pocket for safe keeping as I eyed that dang blasted Sheriff.

"There's been a lynching in Mud Flats Pike," he said, shaking his head back and forth. "Seems the town went plum loco and hanged your brother and sister and all their farm animals. Sorry Pike."

"All their farm animals? What they gonna do that fur?" I said.

Man never quite prepared to hear no news like that. I didn't know what to make of it. Hanging a man is one-thing-but farm animals.

"Well Pike being a Morman town I figure they figured the farm animals where guilty and needed hanging."

"Guilty of what? I said.

"Pike, speaking in tongues. Yep dang blasted Mormons hung the whole lot of um fur speaking in tongues," he said shaking his head back and forth.

I was fit to be tied, first my daddy now my brother and sister and all their farm animals hung. There was only one thing left to be done, and that was to kill everyone dead as ever in Mud Flats and that's what I was gonna do as soon as I got my teeth fixed.

Dr. Bill fixed me up real good; he shoved my two choppers back in my head. Said they would just fall out but he did the best he could do. I saddled my horse and headed fur Mud Flats. There was a whole barrel full of Mormons there, and I was gonna Kill'em all.

Mud Flats were a day's ride out of Silver Dog, down in the low lands. Two big ponderosa pine hills looked down on the town. I made camp on the north side of town with a good view of the place. From my lookout I could count half a dozen houses and a general store.

Those hanging rascals lawed themselves. Hanging people and farm animals alike. If ever there was a town that needed Killin' then Mud Flats were it.

I camped out till it come around Sunday morning. I figured these rascals would have a big social. That way I could get everyone at one time.

I just couldn't figure on how, I couldn't just ride in there and start blasting away without one of them getting away. I had more figuring to do.

I rode on down the hillside until I spotted me a ranch. Seems the rancher was in town socializing with everyone else, that made him fair game.

Being the cowpoke I am, drivng cattle ain't that much of a chore. Once you get them all going in the same direction, that is.

I rounded up two-hundred-head maybe more, not sure. I had a whole dang blasted lot of them I know that much.

I started driving them towards the town. The closer I got the more I drove um hard, getting them worked up good. Being only one road into town and they had set up a long eaten table, just in the center of town.

That's where I aimed my herd-straight on dead center of the whole pack of Mormons and their eaten social.

Now Mormons ain't use to seeing a herd of cattle bearing down on them. They ain't used to anything that ain't of their own making. So for the most part they just stood there dumb-like, watching this stampeding herd barreling in on them.

It didn't take long before two hundred cattle, being driven all out, to make good on pretty much wiping out every cotton picking thing in their way. Women and children don't matter much to cattle.

Within a matter of seconds, the whole cotton picking town was leveled. Whoever had the misfortune of not being stampeded to death, I made quick work of. Like shooting fish in a barrel, everybody running around whopping and hollering, smashing into each other; it was the dangest thing I ever saw.

The whole ruckus didn't take no more than five minutes. Doggone Mormons didn't know how to react to being stampeded to death and then shot outright. They had it comin, can't just hang a man and his sister and all their farm animals and expect to go on social like.

I let a few live-those that were half trampled to death any way. Somehow word got out that it was me that wiped out Mud Flats, and they sent down the new sheriff from Silver Dog to oversee the hanging.

Seems Lawson, Frank Lawson done got himself killed outright. Stepped in front of a runaway freight wagon filled with hollering Chinamen. Fitten' end for that sidewinder of a sheriff if ever was.

He just stood there holdin' that dang blasted broken off handle coffee mug, that's what I was told at any rate. Guess a man don't know how to react to a wagon filled with screaming Chinamen barreling down on him.

I ain't one to mince words; after all I am guilty as sin. So Dr. Bill I am thankful and all that, you havin' a mind to come on down and sit with me a spell. Needed to parley with someone before the hanging man has his way. Dang blasted shame who'll be dropping the floor on me. Well Dr. Bill there's not much I can do about all that, now is there, but wait for that plum loco hangman to do his hanging. For the life of me I just wish that crazy polecat Sheriff Kim Lee puts a cork in all that dang blasted grinning and gets on with it. Can't say I didn't have it comin'. Dang blasted Mormons. I'll see ya around Dr. Bill.

The End

EUGENE WILLIAMS

# A Golfing I will go

    I married my wife because she was the most beautiful woman I had ever seen. She married me to get even with her family. Now if I would have known that at the time, I still would have married; her, after all, love had nothing to do with it.

All anyone would have to do is take a look at me, then my wife, and you'd figure something was rotten in Denmark.

Not that I am an ugly fella, I'm not. Then again who in the dickens would refer to themselves as ugly anyway? Even the ugliest person in the world is somehow convinced that they're not ugly. However, anyone standing within a mile of an ugly person could say" that is one ugly person." I've said it, not about myself of course, about other people, I am sure you have to.

I am sure, no make that positive a lot of people have said that about me. Well before I commit myself to an ugly farm, let me get back to my story.

I have two buddies I grew up with. They enjoy patting me on the back and telling me I am the luckiest fella in the world, grinning at me, then my wife, mostly at my wife. After all, that's what buddies do. I just wish they'd go home every now and then.

I can't blame them for patting me on the back or grinning at my wife or not wanting to go home. After all, I've seen their wives. My colleagues at work are naturally of the opinion that my marriage is all about money. Unfortunately, to the casual observer and those I work with, that money theory doesn't apply to me. Actually, I have a hard enough time paying attention, much less my bills. That has never been the case as far as my wife is concerned. She has the uncanny ability to pay too much attention and spend too much money, but as long as it's hers, I've learned it's better that I don't pay any attention to her money.

People still think it's all about money. Why else would a beautiful woman marry you know someone ugly? Not that I am ugly.

Where was I? As I was about to say, I met my wife on a company business trip as a sales rep for the John Deere Tractor Works in Waterloo, Iowa. I get to travel around to various places, some absolutely fascinating and mind boggling, and others you barely can escape with your life from. El Segundo comes in mind, in the latter category.

About ten years ago, I was at a convention in Boston, Massachusetts, which falls into the fascinating place category. Duck boats and bake beans go pretty well as far as I am concerned. I am sure a few vacationers sitting next to me in the duck boat would disagree, but this isn't about them.

As I was saying, this beautiful young lady introduced herself to me, at the Boston Convention Center, where the convention was being held, which makes perfectly good sense. I've tried to explain this convention thing to my two buddies, but all they seem to be interested in is grinning at my wife.

As I was saying, this beautiful lady told me her father owned about a million acres in Scotland, and they wanted to purchase some farming machinery.

A million-acre farm is rather large, even by Iowa standards. I figured we weren't talking about one tractor and a used backhoe. This was what every sales rep calls the big deal. Literally The Big Deal!

I did the whole spiel and impressed her to no end. We went to dinner and got married, before the convention ended and without her family knowing about it, Nevertheless, what is done is done. There really wasn't a whole lot they could do about it but accept the fact they had a new son-in-law.

Over the last ten years I have received about a dozen threatening phone calls, all in Scottish, which is extremely nerve racking for someone in Iowa. Her father didn't buy any farming equipment from me or anyone working for John Deere. The Big Deal got away. In addition, I am no longer a sale Rep. But I am still married, funny how things work out.

For our tenth, wedding Anniversary my father in-law invited us to spend some time in

Scotland at their million-acre farm. He sent two airline tickets to us.

In addition, he arranged for my wife and I stay at a golfing Hotel in Gullane, Scotland called Greywalls.

I had never heard of Greywalls or Gullane. Moreover, I had never picked up a golf club in my life. Nevertheless, he was trying to reach out, and after ten years of threatening phone calls in Scottish, I wanted to reach out as well- to strangle him, but, of course my wife would have none of that, funny how love just seems to work its way into everything. My father in-law sent some rather strict rules to go along with the airline tickets. How he figured I'd follow them is anyone's guess. I was supposed to master the game of Golf and learn the History of Greywalls and a place called Muirfield links just over the grey stone walls of the place.

My father in-law referred to this Muirfield as the Honorable Company of Edinburgh Golfers, of which he was an honorable golfer. The first thing that came to my mind was la de da, you

Scottish weirdo. Nevertheless, I wanted to check out his million-acre farm. I could care less about Muirfield or Edinburgh. I figured you could put a whole mess of crap on a million acres, and I wanted to see what was on the place. If I had to learn how to play golf-, so be it. How hard could it be, to hit a little ball around a big field with someone driving you from hole to hole, in a cart no less?

After all, golf was for rich and snobby people; everyone knows that. Rich people don't do anything that requires much work. They hire other people to do all the work for them. As far as learning the history of Greywalls, no one is going to ask me about the history of a place I am visiting.

When was the last time someone asked you about the history of a RV park you were staying at? Never. Moreover, if they do, I'll cross that bridge when I come to it.

"Greywalls and Muirfield links can't possible have more history then Pokey's Red Carpet Club, one of the finest golfing and eating' place in Waterloo. How's that for history," I said to my wife. I think she called me an idiot, I'm not, it sounded like idiot.

I looked at my wife, she looked at me. We both looked at the airline tickets and she looked at me again and told me I had one week to master this game of golf and learn how to act like I had some sense. It wasn't going to be easy on either account, and I'm sure she called me an idiot now. She stopped smiling at me and handed me the phone.

"Call Dr. Richards, he plays out at Pokey's every Sunday. He'll show you how to play dear," she said.

The last person I wanted to talk to was my wife's shrink. Not that my is nuts or anything. I think she goes to see him to get away from me.

My wife had been after me for years to go see her shrink, and her shrink has been after her for years to leave me. I really didn't want to call him, but if anyone knew how to play golf, a shrink would so I made the call.

He agreed to set a tee time at Pokey's and pay the green fee. I had no idea I would have to pay to play golf. I thought it was free, just walk out there and start whacking a ball around, turns out is little more to this golf thing then meets the eye.

I arrived early to check the place out. In addition, I asked to leave by some kid in a beanie cap pointing a nine iron at me. I knew this because he took it from me. I tried to explain to him that all I wanted to do was check out his sticks.

I learned quickly that you don't refer to golf clubs as sticks. And you don't touch someone else's clubs. Touchy these golfers to be. I explained I was meeting Dr. Richards after all. "it is a golfing I will go young man," I said. He smiled and did apologize just said, "In that case you can stay Mr. golfer you will go." I had a bad feeling about this kid, but I let it pass.

Dr. Richards shot one hole with me and said, I learned enough that I would do just fine at Greywalls, but there was no way in hell they would let me near Muirfield Links. He began laughing hysterically as he drove off in his cart with me holding my bag of clubs.

I figured this was how it was done so I walked back gave my clubs to the kid in the beanie hat. He took them and called a security guard to escort me to my truck. I figured that was how it was done; after all, rich people like to feel important and all that. I was ready as far as the golf part was concerned: I knew the difference between a Putter and 9- Iron. I knew what a sand trap was and a par. I stopped at the 7-11 figured I'd buy a golf magazine and do a little research. From there I stopped off at the video rental store and rented Caddie Shack. I figured with a movie and magazine and five minutes' worth of golfing I would be ready for Greywalls and the Honorable Company of Edinburgh Golfers La de da. My wife wasn't surprised to see me as soon as I walked in she said." Gus Dr. Richards called he wants to see you in his office as soon as we get back from Scotland."

"I must have impressed him honey," I said.

"He didn't say but he was mumbling something about losing his membership at Porkey's."

Frist thing that came to my mind was the kid in the beanie hat. The owners kid I figured. You know how these rich kids can-be don't take much to get them all butt hurt. I let it pass and slipped in the movie. I figured I'd read the magazine later. My wife woke me up about half way through the movie. I couldn't quite figure out the gofer angle but it was funny.

I paid close attention to the way Bill Murray was swinging at the ball, you know holding his club. After dinner I read the magazine and headed for the bowling alley. Not that I would learn anything about golf there I had to give this golf thing a break for a while can't have too much of a good thing I figured.

It doesn't take long for a week to fly by. My wife began packing our things early. She arranged for our flight out of Waterloo, Iowa to Chicago and from there to New York where we caught our overseas flight to Edinburgh, Scotland.

I brought along the golfing magazine and my wife made two calls to Dr. Richards. Before we landed in New York. During the rest of the flight to Edinburgh she slept, and I got drunk. However, I did manage to memorize the whole magazine from cover to cover. I woke my wife and told her. "I know more about golf than golf knew about me I would dazzle those Scots and beat them at their own game." I think my wife called me an idiot again and fell back to sleep. Not sure it sounded like idiot. I let it pass.

I had never met my wife's father in person but I knew his voice well. He greeted us at the airport in a limousine. I guess he wanted to impress me. It did, and he didn't.

We hadn't gone two blocks from the airport before he started giving me the third degree in Scottish. Puffing away like there was no tomorrow on a Sherlock Holmes pipe, blowing the awfulest smelling tobacco right into my face.

He said. "Twill it yer laddie in a noreastern blinten ears pined 280 meters no way laddie yer be running ni 80 meters blind, yer Iron won't fix yer right. 'Tis yer mum's arse be blinten like doodles she goat, Ni laddie."

"What did he say!" I asked my wife, waving a cloud of smoke out of my face?

"Daddy wants to know what club, would you use to hit your ball 280 meters in a wind coming out of the Northeast dear to leave yourself with 80 meters to the hole and you must have a nice mom."

"That's not what he said! Nevertheless, tell daddy I use my 8-Iron on the ball and my 5-Iron on him if he's not careful,"

"Daddy understand American English really well dear."

"Blinten piggy nip yer ears up, 'tis shank right laddie!"

"What did he say?" I asked.

"Daddy wanted to know if you liked farm animals."

"That's not what he said and you know it!"

"Twill be a lassie niggling yer goo laddie T'day rumpling yer arse Twill ye bloody cup rings."

"What did he say?"

"Daddy wants to know how you feel about women."

"You're kidding right."

"Daddy never kids Gus."

"Ask Daddy if there's any Scotch in this bucket, after all, I've had about enough of daddy."

That pretty much ended my conversation with Vera's father. We traveled on along the ocean through some rather impressive country side. I think he called this part of Scotland East Lothian and these hills were Lammermuir something or other, it was impossible to understand a word he said. Daddy just puffed away on his pipe and gave me the evil eye as we traveled toward this Greywalls

I didn't care anymore about his million-acre farm. He said that the next we came to Scotland; we would be staying with them on the farm. At least that's what my wife said he said. It sounded more like when pig fly and he wanted me to get run over by a cement mixer. I tried to ignore him but my wife was having the time of her life.

My wife and her father, however went on and on about this thing or that. How much the family missed her, and how wonderful it would be if she moved back to Scotland. It was Vi this and Vi that finally I had to ask who in the hell is Vi.

They both looked at me, and my wife said its short for Vera. I said I knew that and I tried to ignore them. I think her father called me a pig sucking idiot, at least it sounded like that; it's hard to say, not even a Scotchman can understand another Scotchman from what I'm told.

They went about how much she was going to enjoy her weekend at Greywalls, how daddy had arranged for a private butler to see to our every need. I wondered if his name was James, but I didn't say anything. Her father was turning a deep purple every time he looked at me.

I just stared back at him to let him know I wasn't very happy about not seeing the million-acre farm; I could careless Greywalls and the butler.

I fiddled around in the compartments of the Limousine until I found a bottle of Scotch and went to work on it. Her father glared at me and packed his pipe full, I guess it was time for round two.

After about an hour we pulled up in front of Crescent Moon shaped building. If I had to describe the place, it. was covered in a honey colored stone, and Ivy climbing up along the walls. Our driver pulled around in front of a door in the center of the building, next to what looked like a baseball cut in half in the center of the drive, just two large half round pieces of lawn with a stone walkway down the middle.

The driveway was some kind of red crushed gravel and every inch of the place was as clean and well-kept as a whistle, this was not your average motel 6 by any means, this place had class.

I was impressed to say the least; this was not at all what I had expected, I wasn't sure what to expect, but this wasn't it. Daddy decided to have one more go at me.

"Laddie yer be blinten Suzy sun bonnet 'Twill give yer a hour 'Twill Muirfield fans yer arse up a giblet Ni history yer be learn fast laddie sakes yer good totting about!"

"What did he say?"

"Daddy said he hopes you know the history of Muirfield and for us to have a wonderful time."

"That's not what he said!"

Our driver must have read the same book of manners as daddy did. The little shot-off Scottish weirdo tossed our bags onto the gravel driveway and hopped back in the car like it was the thing to do.

I climbed out and gave the place the once over, then put a handful of gravel in my pocket.

Our driver stared at me. My wife whispered something in her father's ear. He got back in the limousine, tapped on his window, and called me over to blow a cloud of smoke in my face.

I figured this was one of those welcome- to - Scotland things. Then again I knew he was just being daddy.

My wife, being the kind of person that wants to be in control, suggested I let her do all the talking, after all, these were here kind of folks; she spoke the language and all that. After Daddy I really didn't want anything to do with her kind of folks, so I agreed and followed her into the Inn. I was to refer to the place as Greywalls Inn not motel 6.

Two over bearing senior citizens rushed us as if we had pudding on our luggage, grabbing up our bags and disappearing before I knew what had happened. For a minute there I thought for sure we were just robbed by two geriatric

Scottish fellas in skirts. I started to chase after one of them when my wife grabbed my arm and said it's their job.

Job or not when two ninety-year-old fellas in skirts grabs your luggage and takes off without a word, you naturally want to defend yourself- never know what might happen next.

Our personal butler showed up, introduced himself to my wife, and ignored me. Instead of offering me his hand, he suggested I wait in the library until our room was ready. Considering Daddy hired the fella, I let his rudeness pass.

The Library of Greywalls. Try saying that with a straight face. Was a bit much, to say the least? Frist thing I noticed was a big fat gray cat curled up in front of the fireplace and another one sitting in a red velvet high back chair looking at me. There must have been a thousand books of various sizes along the walls and just as many framed pictures of golfers and clubs and balls and all sorts of golfing do-das all over the place. I walked around checking out the joint like any vacationer would. Picking up books, pretending

I knew what the devil they were about. I checked out the old farts in the photos with their silly little hats and knickers or plus-4, I couldn't remember exactly. Just when I enough of the Library of Greywalls, I hear this squeaky little voice behind me.

"Twill take three damn fine shots ta git in two T'day laddie"

I turned around and three old farts was sitting on a sofa looking at me; where they came from is beyond me. I can't believe I didn't see them there.

"Sorry I don't speak Scottish," I said looking at them looking at me.

"Laddie you do speak English now don't you?"

I figured this one must be the ring leader, considering the other two was grinning

"Of course I speak English you old fart!" I said.

This brought on a round of laughter from the trio; the ringleader stood and offered his hand." I be Colonel McGreger, and this gentleman here be Sir McBeady of Edinburgh, this here be the right honorable lordship McDonnell. And whom you be laddie?" And nodding their heads.

"My friends call me Gus fellas, good to meet you."

"Pleasures all ours. Gus it be? Now Gus what brings you to Greywalls summering, are you not?"

"My wife father set the thing up."

"That be Sir Johnston if I am right."

"That's the one, Mister McGreger, he likes to be called daddy."

Again the three old farts started up with the laughing. Seemed like these three where having way too much fun considering the youngest one McBeady had to be pushing eighty.

"Plan on playing the Links at Muirfield laddie" the fella called McDonnell, said

Before I could answer him, all three broke out laughing again rolling back and forth on the sofa.

"What the hell is with you three?" I said.

"Now laddie, we be pulling your leg; don't take his lordship to heart. You do play the links, now don't you laddie?" McGreger said.

"Doesn't everyone? Why else would I be here ready to play at Muirfield? You think I came here for the women?

Again the tree old farts started up with the laughing. I was beginning to think that everything I said would set them off.

"Laddie, mind if we ask you a few questions?" McGreger said, elbowing his comrade in the side, nearly knocking the old fella off the sofa.

"Fire away, Greger, old boy."

"Who won the 1895 British Open and what course was it played at laddie?"

"You're kidding right." I said eyeing the three musketeers. Eyeing me.

"Standard question laddie they'll as at Muirfield, if you don't know, you can't play."

I thought for a second. Trying to remember if I read about the British Open in my magazine. Yes, I had it.

"St. Andrews, J.H Taylor, you old fart," I said walking around like a peacock.

My turn McGreger, "McBeady said, pulling himself up out of a hole worn in the sofa, probably from him sitting in the same spot for the last fifty years.

"Name Great Golfing Triumvirate laddie, one of them you already did laddie."

I thought for a minute, walking back and forth with my hands behind my back. Stopping on my heels, spinning around and looking at the three old geezers. Shaking my head back and forth, continuing to pace, I could hear them whispering, "he doesn't know, we got him." I turned on them and said with great speed and confidence since I had just read who they were two hours before, but they didn't need to know that. "Harry Vardon, James Briad, and J.H Taylor you old geezers. How's that pay up."

I had them on the ropes now, all three collapsed back on the sofa. They weren't laughing now, but I could see they were planning another attack.

I slowly walked over and began petting the cat by the fireplace. Looking over my shoulder at the three whispering, between themselves I could see they were breaking, slowly breaking. I had the old farts right where I wanted them.

"What's the cat name," I said

I startled them; they weren't expecting a direct question from me.

"Laddie that be Puss you been stoking like a virgin, and the other be Boots," Beady said.

"Now ain't that original?" I said. "I thought for sure you have some kind of Scottish name for Pete's sake, Puss and Boots, that what I call my cats."

"Laddie McGreger chimed." I have another question for you."

I was getting tired of their questions; it was time to bring some life to this party. I could see McDonnell dosing off.

"Fire away Pops."

"Do you prefer the St. Andrews swing or the Vardon?"

"Neither, I prefer the Fling swing." I said stepping away from Puss.

"The Fling swing you don't say. Have you ever heard of the Fling Swing, McDonnell?"

"What was that you say McGreger, swing fling?"

"Not swing fling, governor, Fling swing."

"Never heard of a fling swing. Perhaps laddie will give us a go of it."

"I'll need a club for this fellas." I said walking around the room until I spotted the perfect victim. I pulled a wooden driver off the wall the old boys nearly craped their skirts when I walked back to them. McDonnell tried to pull himself off the sofa, reaching for the club.

"Laddie, put that back. Laddie that belonged to Bobby Jones, old boy. It's priceless, you can't play with that. Return it to its caddie laddie; we be all paying the devil if you break it."

"Settle down before you have a stroke, old boy." I said. Waving the club at him." I won't break the thing. Just a demonstration. Watching and learn fellas how a real golfer golfs."

I got myself into the perfect Bill Murray stance, lifted the wooden club over my head, bringing down the head of the club slowly, balancing it out in front of me. The old fellas were on the edge of the sofa, starring at the club as if it was made of gold. I checked the wind direction with my index finger. They looked at each other.

I brought the club up again, moving it slowly around. They were on the edge of the sofa, three really old men straining to get a good look at what I was doing; the suspense was more than they could take.

With a quick backwards motion, I produced the perfect Fling swing. It was mesmerizing watching the three collapse in absolute shock as the wooden driver left my hands. Flying through the air across the library like an arrow, it found it's mark quite unintentionally.

The wooden driver sailed right into Puss lying by the fireplace; she let out a scream, leaped about ten feet straight up in the air, and fell flat on her back in the middle of the room with her feet sticking straight up. McBeady passed out.

McGreger fell off the sofa, and his lordship let out a cry for mercy, jumped to his feet and ran towards the cat.

"You've killed our pussy with Bobby Jones woody," McDonnell yelled.

I started slapping McBeady back to life, after I helped McGreger off the floor.

His lordship was bent over the cat giving it mouth to mouth resuscitation. Finally, Puss came to life, jumped up, and raced out the room with Boots hot on its trail. That's when my wife walked in.

"Our room is ready," she said looking at the four of us and the broken driver stuck in the bust of Bobby Locke. The wooden head hung out his mouth and swung back and forth.

The airplane ride back to the states was a quiet one; my wife spent the whole time on the phone with Dr. Richards, and I wasn't allowed to get drunk. Funny how love works its way into everything.

No matter how many times you apologize for ruining your wife's vacation, it will never be enough. I'll always remember the five minutes I spent at Greywalls, and I am sure daddy and Greywalls will never forget me.

Some folks were created to play along with the Masters; other to stay as far away from the British Open as possible. Fall in with the latter. Except in my case, my wife has made it perfectly clear she'll go home to daddy, if I ever so much as utter these words again. "A golfing I will go"

## EUGENE WILLIAMS

Printed in Great Britain
by Amazon